THE EYE IN THE GRAVEYARD

BY MICHAEL DAHL

ILLUSTRATED BY FERNANDO MOLINARI

Librarian Reviewer
Laurie K. Holland
Media Specialist

Reading Consultant
Elizabeth Stedem
Educator/Consultant

D1146554

Raintree is an imprint of Capstone Global Library Limited, a
company incorporated in England and Wales having its registered
office at 7 Pilgrim Street, London, EC4V 6LB – Registered
company number: 6695582

"Raintree" is a registered trademark of Pearson Education
Limited, under licence to Capstone Global Library Limited

First
First
T

Art Director: Heather Kinseth
Cover Graphic Designer: Brann Garvey
Interior Graphic Designer: Kay Fraser
Edited in the UK by Laura Knowles
Printed and bound in China by Leo Paper Products Ltd

ISBN 978-1406212693 (hardback)
13 12 11 10 09
10 9 8 7 6 5 4 3 2 1

ISBN 978-1406212839 (paperback)
14 13 12 11 10
10 9 8 7 6 5 4 3 2

British Library Cataloguing in Publication Data
Dahl, Michael.
The eye in the graveyard. -- (Library of doom)
813.5'4-dc22
A full catalogue record for this book is available
from the British Library.

TABLE OF CONTENTS

The Library of Doom is the world's largest collection of strange and dangerous books. The Librarian's duty is to keep the books from falling into the hands of those who would use them for evil purposes.

Molinari '02

CHAPTER 1

THE HEAVY BAG

Ghostly moonlight shines on a vast **graveyard**.

A thin shadow moves through the graveyard, bending the grass.

It is the Librarian. He drags a heavy bag behind him.

A dark bird sits on a gravestone. Its eyes shine like drops of **ink**. Carefully, it watches the Librarian pass.

The Librarian wipes the sweat from his forehead. Tired, he leans against a tall gravestone.

He looks down at the name carved into the stone. He reads <u>Here Lies the First Librarian.</u>

The Librarian bends down and then grabs the bag again.

Inside the bag is something heavier than anything he has carried before.

It is an 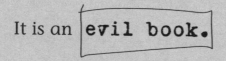**evil book.**

He has brought the book here to bury it.

CHAPTER 2

THE GLASS EYE

The Librarian looks across the **graveyard**.

He sees five dark shapes above the grass.

At the top of the tallest shape is a `bright`, round eye.

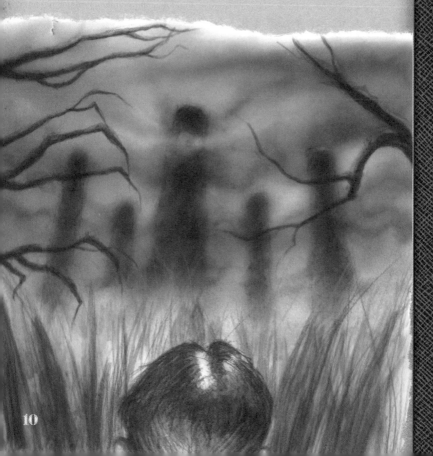

The Librarian has heard stories about the Eye of the Graveyard.

From one of the stories, the Librarian remembers strange words:

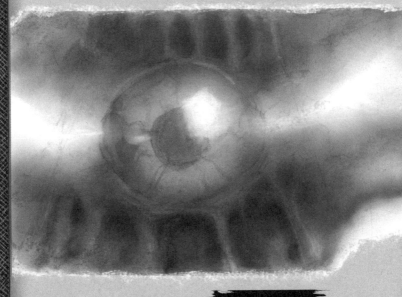

"To escape the darkness

A man must lose his eye."

The Librarian's bag grows
heavier. It falls to the ground.

A cloud passes in front of the moon. The bright eye grows dim and disappears.

Behind him, the Librarian
can hear the black bird croaking.

The Librarian moves closer
to the tall, black shapes .

The cloud drifts away from
the moon.

The eye opens again. It **gleams**
like silver.

The Librarian laughs to himself. The eye is really a glass window in a **high** tower.

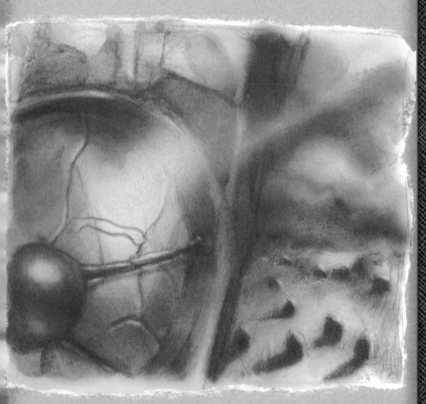

CHAPTER 3

INTO THE TOWER

The Librarian stops smiling. This tower is the one he has been looking for. The evil book will be buried inside the tallest of the five towers.

The book grows **heavier**
inside the bag.

The Librarian can barely drag it through the door in the tower's side.

Steep, curving stairs lead down. At each step, the book inside the bag hits against the stone.

Boom! Boom!

Echoes shake the shadows.

The Librarian reaches the last step at the bottom of the tower. He is dripping with sweat.

He drops the bag and looks around him.

He is standing at the entrance to a gigantic tomb.

A  for books.

CHAPTER 4

THE SINKING

The Librarian takes two gloves from his belt and puts them on. Then he pulls the dangerous book from its bag.

In the center of the tomb is a stone table. The Librarian sets the book on the table and (chains) it into place.

The Librarian stares at the evil pages. He takes a deep breath. The book can never leave this place.

It will never **harm** anyone again.

Then the table shakes. The tomb **shudders.**

The book is 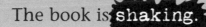 **shaking**.

It breaks its chains and snaps the locks. The stone table is **crushed** beneath the book's great weight.

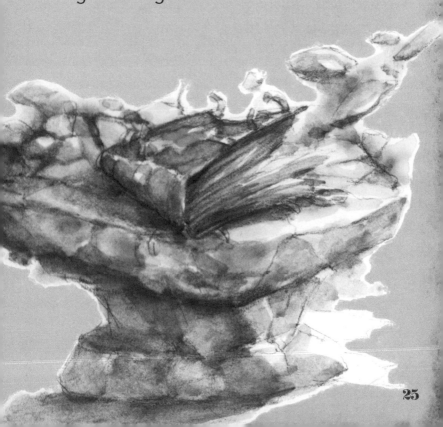

Then the **tomb shivers** again.

The graveyard tower is sinking!

The evil book is pushing it deep into the ground.

Quickly, the Librarian races up the stairs. He can feel the tower sinking beneath his feet.

If he doesn't reach the door soon, he will be **buried alive** inside the tower.

He reaches the top of the stairs,
but he is too late. The doorway has
sunk below the ground.

Worms and bugs fill the space.

He is **trapped** inside.

CHAPTER 5

LOSING THE EYE

The Librarian hears a croak.
He looks up and sees a bird's shadow
on the wall high above him.

Where does the **shadow**
come from?

The Librarian remembers
the window, the glass eye. He
remembers the words of the story.

"To escape the darkness

A man must lose his eye."

The Librarian runs up the
stairs of the tower as it sinks
into the graveyard.

He reaches the top.

He covers his face with his
arms. He throws himself against
the window.

It shatters into a thousand pieces.

The eye is lost.

The Librarian has escaped the **darkness.**

With a horrible rumble, all
five towers sink into the ground.

Weary and wounded, the
Librarian lies nearby. He turns
over on his back to face the sky.

A breeze blows through the graveyard. The **black sky** begins 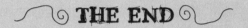 to turn blue.

Somewhere, a bird begins to **sing**.

⟋⟍◉ THE END ◉⟋⟍

A PAGE FROM THE LIBRARY OF DOOM

pitaphs (EP-ih-tafs) are the words found on a gravestone or memorial that tell something about the person buried there. Here are a few.

Underneath this stone
Lies poor John Round,
Lost at sea and never found.

First a cough
Carried me off,
Then a coffin
They carried me off in.

Here lies what's left
Of Lester Moore,
No Les
No more.

Here lies Pecos Bill,
He always lied
And always will,
He once lied loud,
He now lies still.

ABOUT THE AUTHOR

Michael Dahl is the author of more than 100 books for children and young adults. He has twice won the AEP Distinguished Achievement Award for his non-fiction. His Finnegan Zwake mystery series was chosen by the Agatha Awards to be among the five best mystery books for children in 2002 and 2003. He collects books on poison and graveyards, and lives in a haunted house in Minneapolis, USA.

ABOUT THE ILLUSTRATOR

Fernando Molinari was born in Argentina and has worked as an illustrator and art instructor. He has illustrated magazines, CD covers, comics, graphic novels, and books (including Anne Rice's Lasher). His artwork has been shown in various galleries and museums throughout the United States, as well as in The Museum of Modern Art in Buenos Aires. Molinari has won numerous awards and has also appeared on TV to discuss his art and demonstrate his techniques.

GLOSSARY

croak (KROHK) – a deep, scratchy cry or call

gleam (GLEEM) – to shine

rumble (RUM-buhl) – a low noise that sounds like thunder

shatter (SHAT-ur) – to break into lots of smaller pieces

shudder (SHUD-ur) – to shake quickly with fear

vast (VAST) – very big, or gigantic

DISCUSSION QUESTIONS

1. Why do you think the Librarian drags
   the book inside a bag instead of carrying
   it by hand?

2. The graveyard is a creepy place, but is
   it dangerous? Why or why not? Is there
   anything in the story that gives you a
   clue that the Librarian might get into
   trouble in the graveyard?

3. When the Librarian is trapped in the
   tower, he looks up and sees the shadow
   of the bird. The shadow reminds him of
   the window. Do you think the bird was
   trying to help the Librarian on purpose?
   Why or why not?

WRITING PROMPTS

1. The book inside the bag is evil, but we don't know *how* it is evil. What makes the book so dangerous? What happens to people when they read it? Write your own ideas about the heavy book.

2. What would have happened if the Librarian had never jumped out of the window? Would he be trapped forever? Or would he have found another way to escape?

3. Read the epitaphs on the page from the Library of Doom. Then write your own epitaph for an imaginary person who has died. It can be funny, serious, or even scary.

MORE BOOKS TO READ

This story may be over, but there are many more dangerous adventures in store for the Librarian. Will the Librarian be able to escape the cave of the deadly giant bookworms? Will he defeat the rampaging Word Eater in time to save the world? You can only find out by reading the other books from the Library of Doom...